A Silver-Grey Death

银灰色的死

&

Drowning

沉沦

Yu Dafu

郁達夫

Translated By Richard Robinson

Sunny Lou Publishing Company
Portland, Oregon, USA
http://www.sunnyloupublishing.com

Publication Date: November 11, 2023

ISBN: 978-1-955392-43-3

* * *

The translation of *A Silver-Grey Death* from Chinese is based on 银灰色的死 by Yu Dafu (郁达夫), written in 1920 and first published in the "Learning Lights" Supplement of the *News of the Times Newspaper,* Shanghai, July 7, 9, 11, and 13, 1921.

The translation of *Drowning* from Chinese is based on the revised edition of 沉沦 by Yu Dafu (郁达夫), published April 9, 1921.

Contents

A Silver-Grey Death..................................7

    Chapter 1...7

    Chapter 2...17

    Chapter 3...31

Drowning..35

    Chapter 1: Pitifully Lonely.......................35

    Chapter 2: Melancholy..........................43

    Chapter 3: His Hometown.....................49

    Chapter 4: Nagoya...............................55

    Chapter 5: The Naked Eve.....................65

    Chapter 6: Depression..........................79

    Chapter 7: The Japanese Tavern.............85

    Chapter 8: Motherland, Oh Motherland!...95

A Silver-Grey Death

银灰色的死

A Silver-Grey Death

Chapter 1

Yuki's Tokyo was a bit busier than usual. A gentle breeze was blowing down on the city from the summit of Mt. Fuji, but it never completely succeeded in cooling men and women's ardent moods. That time of year was quickly rolling around again when one thousand nine hundred twenty years ago a star appeared in Bethlehem's sky. That time of year when all the shops in the streets and small alleys are decorated like newlyweds, and several shops do their utmost to attract as many customers as possible, in order to increase their year-end profits; that time of year when both rich and poor have the same sense of urgency. A time of saying farewell to family and friends, a time of endless sadnesses.

Near Shinobazu Pond in Ueno, amidst a chaotically arranged group of houses, there was one house, several stories tall, standing in the clear and bright winter air. The family that lived there seemed completely oblivious to this busy end-of-the-year activity outside, having shut themselves in upstairs, their windows tightly shuttered and their doors locked. At this time of the day, the golden sun had already lifted itself up out of Ueno's woods and was suspended in the middle of an ocean-blue sky, gently smiling down on humanity in its hustle and bustle.

When the sun's light, from a slit in the tightly closed door, obliquely fell onto his pillow, it made that pair of eyes, like two walnuts, open; he was about twenty-four or twenty-five years old already. Inside the pitch-black room, the ray of light, reflecting on his eyes deeply set in their sockets, made his complexion look even more ashen in appearance than it really was, under the rather high cheek bones on either side of his face; he was in fact a very lean person.

He half-opened one eye, glanced at the clock on the nightstand, where both hands were pointing to the Roman numeral "X"; he opened his mouth and let out a yawn; he had no idea that he was the protagonist of a major tragedy; he continued to lie in bed for a while, half awake, half dreaming, while making a kind of hissing sound. Hearing the wall clock next door strike eleven o'clock, he sprung up out of bed. Hastily putting on some clothes, by picking up the first thing that came to hand, he ran downstairs, washed his face and hands, slipped on a pair of worn-out leather shoes, and ran outside.

His current lifestyle was quite different from what it had been, in a another place; since the end of October until now, within the span of about two months, he was in the habit of staying up late and going out to drink to each and every tavern that he stumbled across. In Tokyo's taverns the hostesses are all sixteen- and eighteen-year-old girls. Although he knew that they all thought they could cheat him out of his money, and it was for this reason that they agreed to joke with him, to play with him, nevertheless when the sun went down in the west, he never felt comfort-able staying at home alone. Sometimes he thought about correcting this bad habit, so he made his way to the library where ordinarily he loved studying books, but by the time he arrived they were already lighting the lamps [in the taverns], and suddenly he could hear in his mind all sorts of sorrowful ballads being sung. In his nostrils was the smell of cosmetics, sesame oil, fried fish, cigarette smoke, and strong alcohol mixed together with sweet fragrances. Between the lines of the characters on the page a red- and white-painted face suddenly appeared. An enchanting pair of eyes slowly grew larger. Lips like a Japanese rosebud gradually blooming, with two little dimples becoming visible. He could make out a row of white enamel teeth. He closed his eyes, and already he could see be-fore him a number of charming women sitting in the reflection of the red lights. Some looked back at him with sidelong glances, some nodded their head at him, some took off all their clothes, some reached out to him with their soft white hands. When things got to this point, it was always the same: he could not help unconsciously taking that delicate hand in his own and running off with it, as if in a dream. By the time the warm and soft physical body of the girl whose hand he was holding in his mind was sitting beside him, then he knew he was no longer in the library.

Last night, he was again sitting in a tavern like this one, until well past one o'clock in the morning, when he finally walked out; he was in a confused state of mind at that moment, staggering left and right on the road for a while, looking all around but unable to spot so much as shadow of a human being. The countless houses were all closed and silent at that hour, with only a row of irregular door lamps casting their yellow light into the hazy darkness of the street. In the middle of the street were two electric tramcar wires which seemed to emit a phosphorescent blue light. He stopped walking, leaned against the university's iron railing[1], lifted his head to see the bright moon in its thirteenth night of the month, like a silver flower pot floating in the pale blue sky. He took a long look around him again and only then did he notice, on the quiet electric tramcar tracks, on the electric post, on the electric wires, on the crooked rooftops, the moonlight sprinkled like frost. He thought of himself as a very lonely person, like a sailor one meets who has just returned from the stormy sea, like someone wandering alone in the snow at the North Pole. Exhausted, leaning his back against the iron railing, he looked up at the moon. He gazed at it for a long while, with those two lazy old dog eyes of his, when suddenly two tears dropped. Last summer, scenes of when he was married, like a carousel, turned round before his eyes.

High and low mountains on three sides, on the fourth an open expanse, and what smelled like river water in the air. In the middle of the mountain range was a plain, which with its vast emptiness gave the onlooker, at first sight, a kind of eerie feeling, knowing that below the sky there was a river. Where the mountainside ended, in the middle of the area where

---

[1]University's iron railing...: most likely the University of Tokyo, the first Imperial University of Japan, founded in 1877, located just west of Ueno Park's Shinobozu Pond; the author, Yu Dafu, studied political economics there from 1916-22.

the field began, were some houses, bordering which was a meandering blue rivulet that ran through a thin copse of trees and creeping vines. In a deeply emotional and dreamy summer, as he was lying in bed with his bride; he got up again from the bed, because the weather was extremely hot, and walked over to the open window that faced the creek in order to breathe in some fresh air. The lights had already been put out, and the moonlight shot into the room through the window. Sitting down in a rattan chair, he looked at the moonlight as it fell onto his wife's face. He stared at her face for long time and, for the life of him, he could not tell it apart from a sculpture in white marble. Finally, he began to grow afraid in his mind, and unconsciously he reached out with his right hand to touch her face.

"How can your face feel so cold?" he asked softly.

"It's not important, it's nearly midnight, and other people are already sleeping: don't wake them."

"I'm asking you, ah! how can it be that your face has no color to it?"

"There you go again; it's about me going to die young!"

After she had said this, he instantly began to feel his eyes welling up with warm tears. Without knowing why, he then reached out with both his arms and held her tightly. While his lips were pressed against her cheek, he felt two streams of tears flowing down her face. They both sobbed for a long while, flesh pressed against flesh; when he felt his chest gradually begin to relax and he began to feel better, he fixed his gaze out the window again and saw everything far and near completely bathed in bright moonlight. Looking up at the sky, which was vast and hazy, he saw a very thin wisp of light floating and wavering there.

"Look at the Milky Way, it...."

"Probably at one edge of it, that really small star there, that's my birth star."

"Which star is that?"

"Vega."

After having said this, they both stopped talking and didn't say another word. They both silently sat there for a while, him straining his eyes to see that little star, [her sitting up in bed]; and then in a low voice he said to her:

"Next year I may not be able to come home; I'm afraid that you will suffer more than that Vega star endures."

Leaning against the university's iron railing, feeling exceptionally numb now, standing there in the moonlight, he recalled this past event. As soon as he remembered that conversation, his eyes welled up with tears, and he wept, repeatedly and continuously, as the tears streamed down his face. In his mind, he remembered the small window that faced the stream, the frame of the window, the lacquered surface of the table. He remembered a sheet of half-light emitted by the never-dying kerosene lamp on the table; the light fell on a girl of about twenty years old, who was sitting up in bed; that girl's wan complexion, her two big, fascinating eyes, the curved line of her small thin, ashen lips, were all reflected in his memory. Then he said to himself:

"She's gone, she's really gone... gone forever, that telegram [I received] on October 28, it's true... that letter at the beginning of the month, on November 4, forever true... the poor thing! when she was coughing up blood and breathing her last breaths, she called out my name."

The tears were flowing when he straightened up and began to walk away from the iron railing; the effect of the alcohol was beginning to wear off, and as a result he began to feel just how cold it was outside. Although it was the dead of night now, he was as yet unwilling to return to his hellhole of a lodging. As it turns out, he was a lodger at a friend's house; he lived upstairs, without a fire bowl or heat, just some old books spread out waiting for him in the dim yellow light of a single electric bulb; the more he thought about it, the more unwilling he was to return home, so he walked very slowly in the direction of Ueno's train station[2]. Actually, at Japan's train stations, workers work throughout the night and don't sleep; they hang around in the waiting room where there is a fireplace; he was going to go to the train sta-

---

[2]Ueno's train station (上野駅): once an important station where steam locomotives came and went, connecting Tokyo with the snowy northeastern areas of Japan. Today it is the modern train station just east of Ueno Park.

tion, and he was thinking to go in and warm himself by the fire.

He walked directly to the train station; in the chilly streets, not a soul did he meet; he entered the train station, and in the long hallway, empty and quiet, he saw only two rows of electric lamps emitting their yellow light. In the ticket office, two or three female workers were sitting and yawning. He entered the second-class waiting area and, as he sat there for two hours, half awake half asleep, he watched the fire in the fireplace rapidly die down. From far away, he could hear the sound of locomotive wheels turning, as a train made its way to the station. Inside the train station several uniformed employees ran here and there, to and fro, then waited for a while until the train from the northeast arrived. The train station suddenly came alive; there were the footsteps of travelers as they disembarked from the train, and all sorts of shouting and hollering sounds, blended together into one combined sound that reached his ears; together with the disembarked passengers, he exited the train station. On exiting it, he lifted his gaze and saw a deep-blue sky with countless twinkling stars in it; then all of a sudden, from the north, a cool breeze began to blow; he felt that it was intolerably cold. The moon had already gone down behind the mountain. There were a few early-risers on the street, workers who were walking or pulling their cart slowly; each shop door on the street had a light that appeared tired as it continued to emit its feeble light. When he had reached the west side of Ueno Park, he let out a long sigh. In the dim and hazy lamp light, yellow leaves dropped softly from the branches; all around him, the withered trees seemed to come alive; he shivered for the cold, but just stood there silently. Calmly he listened, but for a long while he could not hear a thing, nothing stirred in any direction, except for the distant rumbling sound of the train wheels reaching his ears, intermittently still, as if in a dream, until he finally realized that it was not the train after all, but only the sound of the dead leaves falling. When he walked past Guan Yue bridge[3] he could make out, on the pond's other shore, in the emerging pre-dawn light, a row of tall buildings[4] deep in sleep. The two rows of light there seemed to be taunting him, and when he got home and fell asleep, the Eastern sky had already begun to turn light-grey in color.

---

[3]Guan Yue Bridge: a bridge leading to Bentendo Temple, located on an island in the middle of Shinobazu Pond, in Ueno Park.

[4]Tall buildings: many of which buildings associated with the temple were destroyed in 1945.

Chapter 2

It was another fine day of early-winter weather; at eleven o'clock in the morning, he hurriedly washed his hands and face, slipped on a pair of worn-out leather shoes, then ran outside.

Under the canopy of a deep blue sky, in the soft sunlight, after walking around aimlessly for what seemed like an hour, he was dying of hungry. He patted his pockets and looked into his leather bag: he still had five yuan left. Half a month earlier or so, he had patted himself down as well, but could not find a thing: everything had already been sold for money, so he had no choice but to pawn his late wife's diamond ring. This last keepsake of his late wife was only worth one hundred sixty yuan, which lasted him half a month, of which today he had about five yuan left.

"Late wife, ah late wife, please forgive me!"

He mourned her for a spell, felt ashamed for a spell, but in the end he had to focus on the present and urgent situation at hand. His stomach would not stop growling. He reflected that even with five yuan left he still did not have enough money to get drunk on at a top-quality tavern, so he decided to visit the tavern he often went to when he was out of money.

The owner of that tavern, located near the botanical gardens, was a widow in her fifties; helping her tend the stove was her daughter, who went by the name of Jinger. Jinger had turned twenty years old this year. Her looks were common, but her two eyes like limpid autumn pools of water and her nose, with its high bridge like a white person's, gave her face a look that, for some reason, could not easily be forgotten. Moreover, Jinger had an exceptionally kind nature, always treating everyone equally, and always wearing a smile on her face. These two women, because they did not have a lot of customers, did not employ a cook. Jinger's mother, who had formerly worked in a Western-style restaurant as kitchen help, was versed consequently in some of the secret arts of seasoning. In the past, when he was out of money, he would by and large run to Jinger's place, for one thing because she treated him with great consideration, for another because he was accustomed to going there, not to mention also that Jinger's mother trusted him, and no matter how much he consumed, she always agreed to extend him credit. Whenever he got drunk, he always told the daughter how good his late wife was, how fine, how poorly his mother had treated her, how she had contracted consumption finally and, when she was dying, how she wished him a bright future. Whenever the cemetery was mentioned, tears always welled up in his eyes; Jinger sometimes even cried with him. Although he had been visiting Jinger's tavern for no more than two months, whenever he arrived, Jinger treated him like an old friend of many years; sometimes even she confided in him about some unpleasant event in her own life. According to Jinger, whenever a man or a woman, it didn't matter who, had some secret or some sad situation they were going through, they always wanted a friend, *someone* to console with, that's all they needed to feel better. He and Jinger were probably a pair of friends who could share each other's grief.

Half a month earlier, he had heard a rumor, only he didn't remember where he had heard it, that Jinger "wanted to get married." Because he wasn't willing to ask her directly about it just yet, he merely silently observed her behavior. Because he had this suspicion in his mind, he felt that Jinger's attitude towards him, compared to formerly, had something different about it. One evening as it was getting late, he was at Jinger's place drinking when a man in his thirties came in. Upon seeing this man, Jinger immediately went over to speak with him, abandoning her guest. Because Jinger had left him, he had no other choice but to go over and engage in some idle conversation with Jinger's mother. But while he was engaged in conversation with her mother, he kept an eye on Jinger and that other man. He waited for her for more than half an hour, but Jinger was still completely absorbed, talking and laughing with that other man, until finally he could not take it anymore and, like a wounded animal, walked out of the tavern in a hurry. Since that day until now, for about half a month, he hadn't visited Jinger's place again. After having broken off relations with Jinger, he drank with a much greater ferocity than before, thinking about his late wife and experiencing heightened grief.

"An intimate someone to console and be consoled by, – now where can I find such a friend!"

Recently, after having mourned his late wife, the way things were left with Jinger began to loom in his mind. Sometimes his late wife's face would actually get blended with or superimposed on Jinger's. After having broken off relations with Jinger, he felt even more distressed and lonely. He patted his pockets, looked inside his leather bag, but all he could find were five yuan. He then thought about using this as a pretext and running off to Jinger's place. He thought about doing this on the one hand, on the other hand he remembered a character in *Tannhäuser*,[5] one Wolfram von Eschenbach.

Thinking of him, he then sang two lines of his from *Tannhäuser*:

Dort ist sie; – nahe dich ihr ungestört!...
So flieht für dieses Leben
Mir Jeder Hoffnung schein!

(But you, go and stand beside her skirt, go and clearly consider your mutual debts of yearning!)

(How pitiful I am, all my life, so cold and lonely! You see that famous flower in the mirror, – it's gone again, a wisp in the wind!)

Reading it over several times again, he then said to himself:

"I can go there, there is nothing preventing me from going to her place; in the old days a lover could court her in this way, is it possible that I'm unable to

---

[5]*Tannhäuser:* an opera by Richard Wagner, which deals with the struggle between sacred and profane love.

court Jinger in just such a way?" Looking at it like this, it seemed as though he was trying to justify his behavior to other people; when in fact, apart from his own conscience, nobody was reproaching him. When he had finally walked into Jinger's place, both mother and daughter had just gotten out of bed. Jinger saw him, smiled slightly, then said to him:

"How can you stay away for so long?"

In his mind, he wanted to say:

"You should ask yourself that question!"

But when he saw the gentle expression on Jinger's face, he could not say what he was thinking, so instead he replied like this: "Because I've been very busy of late."

When Jinger's mother heard him say this, she looked at him, pretending to be angry, and said:

"Very busy? Jinger's boyfriend says that you often go to his place recently to drink."

Jinger heard what her mother said and, looking uncomfortable and embarrassed, she blurted out:

"Ma!"

He saw the scene unfolding before his eyes, then he got to the heart of the matter with Jinger's mother by saying:

"And Jinger's boyfriend is who?"

"The owner of the tavern in front of the university, – you didn't know this already?"

Then he turned toward Jinger and said:

"When is your wedding day? Congratulations: I hope that you will very soon give birth to a son. We will have to come and celebrate with you."

Jinger stared at him for a moment without any expression on her face, looking as though she was about to cry. She heard what he had to say, then she asked him, "What do you want to drink?"

He heard her voice, it seemed to be trembling. Suddenly he felt miserable, as if a sad and bitter taste, like a sea-sick person's vomit, was being forced up from his stomach and into his heart. He felt like he had something to say but couldn't get it out of his mouth, he could only nod his head again and again, making it clear that he wanted something to drink. He looked at Jinger, Jinger looked at him, two people's eyes like electric lamps emitting beams of light at the other; then Jinger hurriedly ran outside to buy some food to go with the alcohol.

When Jinger came back, her mother then went down into the kitchen to prepare the food; the food not being ready yet, but the rice wine already warm, Jinger then, as usual, sat down in front of him and poured him his wine, but he never dared to lift his head to look at her, and Jinger also did not dare lift her head to look at him. Jinger also did not dare to say a word, and he just sat there silently drinking. The two of them just sat there dumbly for a while until Jinger's mother finally called out to her from the kitchen below:

"Food is ready, come and get it!"

Jinger heard her, but just sat there motionless. Without thinking, he stole a glance at her; Jinger looked as though she were crying.

He knocked back several cups of rice wine, ate several small plates of food, then he got up and staggered out. Outside on the street, people's voices were very noisy. He passed down a street, then continued walking until he reached a calm road where he took several steps; then, after he had walked up a long slope that was facing West, he saw that the sun was already setting. He turned around and looked into the distance, the tops of the trees in the arboretum all had a crimson-yellow tint to them; the distant mountains on the Western horizon were all saturated with sunlight, and the roofing tiles far and near reflected the dying sun; he didn't know why, but everything seemed reluctant to depart. He stared blankly at the scene for a while, then turned around, so that the remaining light of the dying sun shone on his back, and he walked in an easterly direction up the slope.

As if in a dream, after he had walked distractedly through the main gate of the university, he suddenly heard someone call out his name:

"Master Y, where are you going! Are you staying in Tokyo during the holidays?"

He looked up and recognized one of his former classmates. With a fresh haircut, wearing a new Western-style suit, a rattan traveling case in one hand, he was probably just about to go home for the New

Year. He looked at his classmate and, with a smiling expression on his face, very quickly responded:

"Yes, I'm not going anywhere; are you going home for New Year?"

"Yes, I'm going home."

"When you see your sweetheart, please give her my regards."

"Okay, she's afraid she will miss you too."

"Don't tease, I wish you a safe journey, bye bye."

"Bye bye..."

After his classmate had walked away, he was all alone in the middle of the university campus, at dusk; he just stood there for a long while, without moving, as if he were crazy. Finally, he started walking slowing, while at the same time talking to himself:

"They have all gone home. They all have a family to go to. 哦! 家! 甜蜜的家!"[6]

Automatically, without putting much thought into it, he walked home, went upstairs, sat in the light of an electric lamp for a spell, and ran over again in his confused state of mind what he had just heard at Jinger's place.

"Not bad, not bad, Jinger's wedding day falls in the first lunar month of the new year," he said to

---

[6]哦! 家, 甜蜜的家: oh! home! sweet home!

himself.

He thought things over for a while, then stood up, picked up several old books, bound them together with string, then, calmly and collectedly, carried them to a second-hand book shop in front of the school. After a protracted negotiation for several books of genius in exchange for a measly nine yuan or so in pocket change, he decided to hold onto the collection of English poetry however because the owner of the second-hand bookshop was practiced at the art of haggling and offered him only a meagre sum for it.

To receive only nine yuan or so in pocket change, he felt outraged on the one hand because of the authors' genius that went into writing those books, but on the other hand he was quite satisfied. Because with nine yuan or so in pocket change, he could plan for a night out of eating and drinking to his heart's content, moreover he could attain his greatest goal – which was that he could use some of the money to buy a wedding gift for Jinger.

When he left the second-hand bookstore, it was already twilight in the street; at a shop specializing in women's articles he bought a few beautiful hairbands (ribbons) and two bottles of violet-scented perfume, then he ran directly to Jinger's place with them.

Jinger was not there; her mother was alone, warming herself by the fire; when she saw him come in, Jinger's mother appeared to have a look of loathing on her face. She asked him:

"So it's you again, eh?"

"Where's Jinger?"

"Taking a bath."

On hearing this, he approached her, taking out the hairbands and perfume bottles that he had been concealing inside his jacket, and he said to her:

"These small trifles, please give them to Jinger for me, as a wedding gift."

Jinger's mother looked at those gifts and, smiling now from ear to ear, she said:

"Thank you so much, thank you so much; when Jinger returns, I will tell her to come over and express thanks."

He saw by the color of the sky that it was already evening, then he asked Jinger's mother to warm up a bottle of rice wine for him and prepare some plates of food; by the time he had finished drinking his second bottle, Jinger returned. When Jinger saw him sitting there drinking again, she was surprised, and didn't know what to say; finally she said:

"Ah, you again..."

Jinger went down into the kitchen and walked about for a while, speaking many things with her mother, before returning to his table. He thought she had come to thank him for the gifts, but she didn't say one word about them; instead she just sat down blankly in front of him and poured one cup after the next of the wine for him. Finally, when he did his utmost to convince her to get him some more wine, Jinger's eyes flashed red, and she said to him:

"You should stop drinking now. After all this wine, and you still want more?"

He heard these words of hers, and then drank to his heart's content. In his mind he felt grief and sorrow; he didn't really know what to tell her; on the one hand it seemed like he was exacting revenge on Jinger, on the other hand it seemed like he was mourning his own death.

After laying drunk on Jinger's bed for quite some time, two o'clock in the morning finally rolled around and he staggered out of Jinger's place. The street was empty, and it was covered far and wide with a thin layer of silver-grey moonlight. There was not the faintest sound or activity in any direction except for the distant sound of a barking dog; in all the world it seemed like everything had died. Stumbling here and there as he walked for a while, he suddenly came across a nightstand selling food and drink. He patted himself down and in one of his pockets he found four or five *yuan*, five *jiao*[7] still, of paper money. At the night stand, he was once again drinking to his heart's content. He felt that everywhere, on earth and in the sky, all the buildings and houses were spinning round him. Falling forward and jerking back, he walked in this way for two hours, only to see opening up before him a very broad and empty space. The cool light of the moon together with the dark shadows of every object or thing were lumped together in one

---

[7] *Jiao*: a monetary unit equal to 1/10th of a yuan.

single mass that was reflected in his eyes.

"This here has got to be the medical school for women," he told himself.

By thinking in this way, his mind gained clarity, but then his brain suffered another spasm and he was not himself again. A scene from several days earlier, like stills from a movie picture or film, flashed quickly before his eyes.

The sky was filled with cold, dark grey clouds; a north wind was blowing pressingly; in the shadow of the dead leaves still hanging on the trees, he stood at the entrance to Ueno Park's Seiyōken,[8] and received guests. It was the day of the annual welcoming party for fellow villagers of the W clan; among the people who were coming and going, he caught sight of a seventeen- or eighteen-year-old girl, walking toward the party, taking her time; she was wearing the medical school's uniform, and she was in no hurry. When he saw her face, he could not help but stare. As he waited for her to pass, he was like a man who had just awakened from a dream; in a bit of a flurry, he rushed forward to greet her and said:

"Your hat and jacket, please; take them off and give them to me."

Two hours later, the welcoming party was over. It was about five o'clock in the evening already. At the exit, where people waited for their coats and hats, there was a large crowd. When he came down a

---

[8]Seiyokan (精养轩): built in 1872, it was one of Japan's first Western-style restaurants.

floor, he saw that girl again; she was not wearing her coat yet and was quietly standing there at the entrance; so he went up to her and said:

"Has anyone gone to get your coat?"

"Not yet."

"Give me that copper token, and I'll go fetch it for you."

"Thank you."

In the boundless dim light of the evening, he could see her fine sets of white teeth, and he felt immensely rejuvenated in spirit. After he had gone and fetched her coat and hat, he then ran back and helped her on with the coat. She turned her head to look at him before hurriedly walking out the door. He ran after her a pace and opened his eyes widely so as not to lose sight of her, as her slender shadow faded away into the darkness. Thinking about it, he felt that that fine and delicate body of hers had seemingly just disappeared before his very eyes.

"One moment, please!" he called out to her.

He rushed forward several steps, but then his tall and slender body just fell flat on the ground. The moonlight was shining at an angle. In the empty area before the medical school for women, the darkness grew thicker, and not a sound could be heard in any direction. Over time, the silver-grey light of the moon covered that open space of ground, purifying every single object on earth.

Chapter 3

In the early morning on December 26, the sun rose in the east, as usual; when its rays had lit up the area in front of the Ushigome Ward[9] Office, an old public servant, holding an official notice in his hands, proceeded to paste it onto a notice board. The notice said this:

A traveler in ill-health, twenty-four or twenty-five years old, five feet five inches tall, lean in appearance, with yellow complexion, rather high cheek bones, disheveled hair several inches long, but no other distinguishing characteristics beyond these.

He was wearing a black, Western-style suit. In his pocket was a book, "Ernest Dowson's Poems and Prose," five jiao of paper money, a white silk handkerchief with a woman's initials, "S. S.", sewn on one side of it. A black soft cap on his head, on his feet a pair of yellow, worn-out leather shoes, both damaged.

Cause of illness: cerebral hemorrhage; the body was found at 9 am in the morning, the twenty-sixth day of this month, in Ushigome, as if resting on the elevated path between the cultivated fields in the area in front of the

---

[9]Ushigome Ward: (牛込区) a former ward in Tokyo, prior to 1947.

women's medical school; length of time of decease: approximately four hours; name or address of the deceased, utterly unknown, hence the body was cremated.

– Notice of the Ushigome Ward Office

Drowning

沉沦

Drowning

Chapter 1: Pitifully Lonely

Recently he had been feeling pitifully lonely.

His precocious temperament in fact, – when he came into contact with others, who were not compatible with him in the least, – erected a wall between them and him such that the more he bumped up against them, the taller the barrier grew.

The weather was getting colder with each passing day. It was September 22, already half a month into the new school year.

In a clear blue sky, with not a cloud to be seen for miles around, the bright sun moved slowly along its normal trajectory. From the south a mild breeze blew in small, sudden bursts, carrying with it the fragrance that was like that of a good, bracing, rice wine. Amidst the yellowish green, unripe rice paddies, on the meandering white line of a country road, he was all by himself, walking slowing, holding a pocket-size volume of Wordsworth's poetry in his hands. In that wide-open plain, with not a human soul in sight in any direction, he could hear the sound of one or two dogs barking in the distance, but he didn't know where the sounds came from. Melodiously the sounds reached his ears. He took his eyes off his book, and as if in a dream he looked in the direction of the barking, but he all he could see was a thicket of trees, several houses with roof tiles like fish scales, and a very faint wisp of a mirage, like gauze, floating in the air.

"Oh, you serene gossamer! You beautiful gossamer!" he said to himself.

After speaking out loud like this, his eyes welled up and two lines of pure tears streamed down his face, and he didn't really know why.

Blankly staring into the distance for a long time, he felt a small breeze at his back suddenly, filled with the fragrance of violets, and he stopped to listen; he thought he heard a faint swishing sound somewhere in the bushes along the path – which made him immediately snap out of his dream and whip his head around to look, – there, he saw a small flower still nodding its head, stirred by the warm breeze bearing a fragrance of violets on it, a faint puff of air on that pale face of his.[10] In that clear and warm world of early autumn, in the middle of that clear and transparent air, his body began to feel weak as if he were intoxicated. He felt as if he were sleeping in a warm and caring mother's embrace. He felt as if he was dreaming in the Peach Blossom Spring[11] world. He felt as if he was on a southern European sea coast, reclining, with a strong desire to take an afternoon nap in his sweetheart's lap.

---

[10]The passage has echoes of English and European Romantic literature in it. Wordsworth, Coleridge, Novalis, for instance.

[11]Peach Blossom Spring world, a fable written by Tao Yuanming in 421 CE.

He looked all around, in all four directions, and he considered the surrounding vegetation, – everything there was smiling at him. Looking up at the blue sky, he thought the long and endless natural world was nodding to him faintly. Completely immobile, he stared at the sky for a long while, and he thought that up in the sky there was a group of little gods, with wings on their backs, bows and arrows hanging from their shoulders, dancing. Then, not knowing what he was doing, he opened his mouth and began talking to himself out loud, saying:

"This place truly is your refuge. The common people of the world are envious of you, they quietly laugh at you, and make a fool of you; there's only this natural world, this eternally recurring blue sky and bright sun, this late summer breeze, this early autumn pure air, – they are your friends, your caring mother, your sweetheart; you don't need to go back and co-exist again in the world with those frivolous young boys and girls, just spend your last days here in this natural world's embrace, in this simple and honest country-side!"

Having spoken in this way, he felt pity for himself, as if he had a million resentments running through his heart and mind, that he was unable to expel in one ex-halation apparently. He held back two tears, and his eyes looked down at the book he was holding in his hand.

> *Behold her, single in the field,*
> *You solitary Highland Lass!*
> *Reaping and singing by herself;*
> *Stop here, or gently pass!*

Alone she cuts and binds the grain,
And sings a melancholy strain;
O, listen! for the Vale profound
Is overflowing with the sound.[12]

After reading the first stanza of this poem, he suddenly turned the page and automatically proceeded to
read the third stanza.

Will no one tell me what she sings?——
Perhaps the plaintive numbers flow
For old, unhappy, far-off things,
And battles long ago:
Or is it some more humble lay,
Familiar matter of today?
Some natural sorrow, loss, or pain,
That has been, and may be again?

It was a kind of recent habit of his, while reading a
book, never to read it from beginning to end all at
once. Several hundred pages of a large book, it goes
without saying, but even ten pages from a pamphlet,
like Ralph Waldo Emerson's "On Nature," or Henry
David Thoreau's "Excursions," etc., he never read
them completely from beginning to end at one go. As
soon as he opened a book and began reading it, after
four or five lines or one or two pages, he'd be so
moved by each passage that he felt like swallowing
the book whole; and then, after another four or five
pages, he felt so moved in his heart that he seemed to
say to himself:

"This wonderful sort of book should not be read from
beginning to end in one go, but rather it should be

---

[12]From "The Solitary Reaper," Wordsworth.

mulled over and carefully considered before moving on. Before I know it, I will have finished, and what I so ardently desire will need to come to an end; at that time I will have no more good hope, no dreams, what's the point?"

Although he had these kinds of thoughts, actually he very quickly grew a little weary in his mind, and when he reached that point he always put the book down and could not pick it up again. After several days or several hours had passed, he was filled with enthusiasm again, and he picked up another book with feelings similar to those he had felt earlier in the first book. But the feelings for that first book of several days or several hours previous, he had already forgotten about them.

He let out a huge sigh after having finished reading in one stretch the two stanzas of Wordsworth's poetry, and he suddenly got the idea of translating the poem into Chinese.

"The Solitary Reaper" he thought about it some more, "the title of the poem, 'The Solitary Highland Reaper,' can only be translated like this":

「你看那個女孩兒，她只一個人在田裡，

你看那邊的那個高原的女孩兒，她只一個人冷清清地！

她一邊刈稻，一邊在那兒唱著不已；

她忽兒停了，忽而又過去了，輕盈體態，風光細膩！

她一個人，刈了，又重把稻兒捆起，

她唱的山歌，頗有些兒悲涼的情味；

聽呀聽呀！這幽谷深深，

全充滿了她的歌唱的清音。

有人能說否，她唱的究是什麼？

或者她那萬千的癡話

是唱著前代的哀歌，

或者是前朝的戰事，千兵萬馬；

或者是些坊間的俗曲

便是目前的家常閒說？

或者是些天然的哀怨，必然的喪苦，自然的悲楚。

這些事雖是過去的回思，將來想亦必有人指訴。」[13]

After having translated it in one sitting, suddenly he felt bored, then he laughed at himself and scolded himself:

"What stuff is this; how is it any different from the tediousness of church hymns? English poetry is English poetry, Chinese poetry is Chinese poetry, – what is the point of translating it!"

Reciting verse like this made him unconsciously begin to laugh faintly. Looking around, in every direction, he noticed the sun had already started to set; on the other side of a large field, on the western horizon, was a tall mountain, and floating there, absorbing

---

[13]This is a faithful translation of Wordsworth's poem (as given earlier), "The Solitary Reaper," into Chinese. It adds a single line, that is not in the original, wherein the narrator comments on the lithesome figure of the girl and how "exquisite" she looks.

what remained of the day's light, was a layer of misty, hazy air, as if brewing, reflecting a kind of purplish-reddish color.

While he just stood there, absorbed, looking out into the distance blankly, he heard a cough, and he noticed a peasant behind him suddenly. Turning his head to see, the smiling look on his face turned into a dejected expression, as if his smiling would have frightened someone.

Chapter 2: Melancholy

His melancholy grew worse as he became more agitated.

He felt that his school textbooks were insipid, and he didn't find the least bit of pleasure in them. When the weather was bright and clear, he grabbed one of his beloved literature books and ran off to some deserted place by the water's edge, half-way up the mountain, to gluttonously consume solitude's rich flavor. Completely bathed in silence, where the water reflected the sky, he took in the vegetation, the insects and the fish, and he watched the white clouds and blue sky; he imagined himself being one of those lonesome and proud worthies of a bygone age, a superior and aloof hermit. When he ran into a peasant on the mountain, he acted like Zarathustra[14]; as Zarathustra would have spoken, so he spoke in this mind to the peasant. His megalomania grew in direct proportion to his hypochondria, day after day continuing to increase. Indeed, sometimes he didn't attend his lessons at school for four or five days in a row.

Sometimes, when he went to school, he thought everyone was looking at him, at his appearance. He avoided his classmates whenever and however he could; his classmates' gaze always seemed to harbor evil intentions, shot in his direction from behind his back.

---

[14]Zarathustra: see Neitzsche's *Also Sprach Zarathustra*.

In class, although he sat in the room surrounded by other students, nevertheless he always felt extremely lonely; in thick crowds of people, this type of lonely feeling was even more acute than the loneliness he felt when he was all alone in a cold and cheerless place. Seeing his classmates, each and every one of them there in high spirits listening to the teacher's lesson, he was the only one who, although his body was sitting inside the lecture hall, was floating in his mind with the thunderclouds usually, losing himself in boundless daydreams.

How difficult it was to wait for the bell to sound the end of class! After the teacher dismissed the students, his classmates laughed, talked, and joked amongst themselves, each and every one of them like so many joyful bramblings, right there and then making merry; except for him, all alone with knitted brows, his tongue, which seemed weighed down by a rock weighing a thousand *catties*, didn't move or make a sound. He so wanted his classmates to speak to him or share with him some gossip, but they all stayed in their own individual groups and kept their enjoyment to themselves; as soon as they saw him with that frown on his face, not a single one of them didn't drop his head and rush off, in this way giving him more reason to complain about them.

"They are all Japanese, they are all my enemies; one day I will take my revenge, I will always want to revenge myself on them for their hatred."

When he felt grief and indignation, he always thought this way, but after calming down he couldn't help but ridicule and scold himself:

"They are all Japanese, it's only natural for them to have no sympathy for you; because you want to obtain their sympathy, you blame them, – how is this not your fault?"

Some of his classmates were kind; sometimes someone came to chat and laugh with him; and even though he was extremely grateful in his heart, whenever he wanted to share some words of intimate thought or feeling with that person, he could never get the words to leave his mouth; so there were some classmates who understood his good intentions, but they couldn't help but drift apart from him.

When his Japanese classmates were happily laughing together, he always suspected they were laughing *at* him; in a split second he became red in the face. When they were chatting amongst themselves, if by chance he saw one of them look at him, suddenly he would grow red in the face again, for he thought they were talking about him behind his back. The distance between him and his classmates grew wider with each passing day; his classmates all thought he liked to be alone, so nobody ventured to enter into his life.

One day after class, as he was returning to his hotel, carrying his school bag under his arm, three Japanese students were walking in the same direction. When he was approaching the hotel where he stayed, suddenly two schoolgirls in red dresses appeared before him. In that area outside the city, he had never seen schoolgirls there before, so he looked at those two girls, and his breath grew short. When all four of them together brushed by the two girls, his three Japanese classmates asked them:

"Where are you going?"

Those two schoolgirls replied in a sweet voice:

"Dunno!"

"Dunno!"

Those three Japanese schoolboys all laughed loudly, as if they were awfully pleased with themselves; he was the only one apparently who felt troubled and bashful by how the girls spoke, and he hurriedly rushed into his hotel. Entering his room, he threw his book bag forcefully down onto the woven mat, and then he lay down on the mat. His heart was beating wildly at first; he used one hand as a pillow under his head; and he pressed the other hand against the pit of his stomach, and mocked and scolded himself:

"You're so mean and cowardly! If you're so shy, why do you feel regret? If you feel regret, why didn't you have any courage earlier? You didn't say one word to those girls. 呀, 膽小鬼, 膽小鬼![15]"

Having said this, he suddenly remembered those two schoolgirls' bright eyes. Those two lively pairs of eyes!

Those two pairs of eyes, they definitely revealed an idea of desire behind them. But he thought about it some more seriously and then suddenly burst out:

"You're so stupid! Stupid! Even though they showed some interest, what does it have to do with you? So

---

[15] 呀, 膽小鬼, 膽小鬼!: Oh, coward, coward! The original has these words in English instead of Chinese.

their eyes twinkled amorously, – wasn't that only for the three Japanese boys? Ah! Ah! They already knew, already knew, that I'm Chinese, otherwise why didn't they glance at me then! Revenge, revenge, I will always take my revenge on them."

Having said this, several ice-cold tears suddenly rolled down those fiery cheeks of his. He was extremely aggrieved. That evening, he recorded in his diary the following words:

"What was the point of my wanting to come to Japan; why did I come here seeking knowledge. Since I came to Japan, it is only natural that I should be scorned by the Japanese. China, oh China! Why can't you grow big and strong, I cannot bear it any longer.

"My homeland does not have stunningly beautiful mountains and rivers? My homeland does not have pretty girls like flowers? Why did I bother coming to this island nation in the East Sea?

"Having come to Japan, I have also sunk down; why did I bother to come to this damned school. Those students who came here to study and stayed only five months before leaving, did they not find honor and happiness on their return? These last five or six years have taught me how to pull along. I have suffered untold hardships and amassed some ten odd years of scholarly knowledge, – but when I return to my country, can I be certain I'll be better off than those foreign exchange students who came here and made such a fuss?

"Man lives to be a hundred years old; in his youth he

has seven, eight years at best, – these pure and most beautiful seven or eight years, I have no choice but to fritter them away on this heartless island, pitiful me who am already twenty-one years old.

"Withered, twenty-one year old trunk!

"Cold, twenty-one year old ashes!

"I really ought to improve my diet, I have almost never bloomed in my entire life.

"Knowledge – I don't want it; fame – I don't want it; I just want some 'heart' to comfort me, to appreciate me. An incandescent affection. A sympathy born of this affection! And love born of sympathy!

"What I so want to find is love!

"If there was one beautiful person who could understand my suffering, if she wanted me to die, I am willing.

"If there was one woman, pretty or ugly[16] it does not matter, if she can love me with a sincere heart and proper mind, I am willing to die for her.

"What I so want to find is love of the opposite sex!

"Heaven oh heaven, I don't want knowledge at all, I don't want fame at all, I also don't want any of that useless money; if you can confer on me an 'Eve' in the Garden of Eden, make her body and soul completely belong to me, then I will be perfectly content."

---

[16]Pretty or ugly: see Dostoevsky.

Chapter 3: His Hometown

His hometown was a small city on the Fuchun River, not more than eighty or ninety *li* by flow of the river from Hangzhou. The water of this river, originating in Anhui, flows through all of Zhejiang, is winding, and the scenery along it is ever changing; in the Tang Dynasty one poet praised this part of the river, calling it "a picturesque river." When he was fourteen years old, he asked a teacher to write these four characters[17] on a piece of paper so that he could paste them up on the wall of his study room, because the small window in his study room looked out on the river. Although the room was not large, nevertheless wind and rain, darkness and light, spring and autumn, dawn and dusk, all these changes of weather and scenery transpired just outside the tall Tengwang Tower[18]. In this very small study room he had spent some ten odd springs and autumns, until he went with his older brother to study abroad in Japan.

When he was three years old, his father had passed away; at that time, his home life was an unbearable misery. With great difficulty, his oldest brother finished his studies at W university in Japan, returned to Beijing, took the imperial civil service examination, and was awarded the *jinshi* degree; he was assigned a

---

[17]These four characters: 一川如畫 (a picturesque river).

[18]Tengwang Tower: Tengwang Ge, Pavilion of Prince Teng, (滕王閣).

position in the ministry of law, but in less than two years the Wuchang uprising broke out. At that time, he himself had just graduated the county grade school that he attended and was in the processing of going from one middle school to another. Everyone in his family blamed him for a lack of patience; they said he was too restless; however, the way he explained it, it was because he was different from other students, and he couldn't get along with them or stick to the prescribed way of doing things at school. So after he enrolled at K prefectural middle school, not even half a year later he suddenly switched to H prefectural middle school; he was at H prefectural middle school for three months when the rebellion happened.[19] After he stopped studying at H prefectural middle school, he had no other choice than to return home to his very small study room of before. Two springs later, when he had just turned seventeen years old, he was admitted to a preparatory course at college. This college was located outside the city of Hangzhou, originally founded with money donated by the American Presbyterian Church, so the school was permeated by a kind of harmful, dictatorial regimen, and the students' freedom was reduced to a very small scope, about half the size of the eye of a needle. On Wednesday evenings there was something of a prayer group; on Sundays, not only were they not permitted to go outside and enjoy themselves, – apart from singing hymns and reciting prayers, – they were forbidden to read any other books in their leisure time except those of the New and Old Testaments. Each day, early in the morning, from nine o'clock to twenty past nine,

---

[19]Rebellion: the Wuchang uprising mentioned earlier.

they had to attend worship; if they didn't attend worship, their grades would be lowered. Although he really loved the school's adjoining natural landscape and scenery, nevertheless in his heart there was always a desire to rebel, because he was someone who loved his freedom, and he was very unwilling to obey. After living there for a little less than half a year, the school's cook, with the backing of the principal, unexpectedly started to hit the students. Some of the students refused to go along with it, and went to tell the principal; the principal responded that the students were at fault. He gave the situation some serious thought, decided that it made very little sense in fact, and at once informed the school that he was dropping out; then he returned home, to that very small study room of his again; at that time, it was the beginning of June already.

He stayed at home for three months or more; when the autumn winds started to blow on the Fuchun River, and the green trees on both sides of the river were about to shed their leaves, he got into a boat and sailed down the Fuchun River to Hangzhou. But as soon as he arrived, the stone archway of W high school beckoned him to disembark and see about enrolling in classes again, so he went inside to speak with the principal of the school, Mr. Shi, and related his experience to both Mr. Shi and his wife. Mr. Shi allowed him to join the senior class of students. This W high school was also a religious school actually; the principal, Mr. Shi, was also a muddle-headed American missionary; he examined the school's curriculum and found it to be inferior to that of H prefectural middle school. Together with a very contemptible provost – as it turned out, this teacher was a graduate of H prefectural middle school, – it was a noisy, busy place, and by the second year, in the spring, he dropped out. After having dropped out of W high school, he went to visit other schools in Hangzhou, but none of them could meet his expectations, so he decided not to go back to school.

Right around this time, his eldest brother was compelled to leave Beijing. To tell the truth, his brother was an extremely honest functionary and performed his job at the ministry with extreme incorruptibility and impartiality; moreover, when compared with the majority of other functionaries at the ministry, he had a superior erudition; consequently, he was feared both high and low there. One day the personal friend of a certain deputy chief came to visit him and asked for a position, and he was determined not to give it to him; consequently the deputy chief came up with a scheme whereby a complaint was filed against him, and several days later he resigned his post at the ministry, only to transfer to the judicial branch of government and work there as a prosecutor or judge. His second oldest brother was at this time serving as a military officer in the Shaoxing army; this military-man brother of his had acquired some rather bad habits over the years, spent money like water, and passed most of his time making friends with people of questionable character. None of the three brothers at this moment in time was able to do what each of them wanted; as a result, rumormongers and idlers in that small town where they hailed from said that they all possessed rotten *fengshui*.

When he returned home, he passed all day and all night in seclusion in that very small study room. From his paternal ancestors down to his father, and his eldest brother even, all their books were stored there, which he regarded as his good teachers and helpful friends. He wrote poetry in his journal day after day. Sometimes he employed a florid style of writing, to compose novels, and in his novels he represented himself as a kind of gallant knight; the two daughters of his next door neighbor, the widow, he depicted them as noble ladies; the natural landscape of his hometown, he wrote about it like a pastoral scene; and when he was in the mood, he even made simple foreign language translations of his novels; the more his delusions evolved, the larger they became; the seeds of his depression began to sprout and develop at around this time. He remained at home for half a year, and by the second week of July, he received a letter from his eldest brother, which said this:

"The Judicial Yuan plans to send me to Japan, with the purpose of inspecting judicial affairs there, and I have already been given permission to leave by the president of the Yuan; in a few days a formal command will be issued. Before going to Japan, I plan to return home for a little while. Little brother living at home all by himself is definitely not an excellent idea; this time Dangxie will accompany me to Japan." After receiving this letter, each day he looked forward in his heart to seeing his brother come south again; around the latter part of September, his brother and his wife Dangxie arrived from Beijing. They stayed for one month; then he, together with his oldest brother and his wife, left for Japan.

By the time he arrived in Japan, he had not yet snapped out of his "Dreams of the romantic age," and it took him another half year finally until he sat for and passed the entrance examination at a top-ranked college in Tokyo. This was in his 19th autumn.

Just when classes for the new year had started at the top-ranked college, his eldest brother received notice from the Yuan department head, instructing him to return to China. His brother then placed him in the trust of a Japanese family, and, several days later, he and his wife and their newborn daughter returned to China. The top-ranked Tokyo college had a preparatory course of study designed specially for Chinese students. He would be in this preparatory course of study for one year, and after completing it, he would then be able to enroll in any of the school's main classes, together with the Japanese students. After having passed the entrance exam for the preparatory course, he registered himself as a literature major, but later as he was in the middle of his course of studies, his brother insisted that he change his major to medicine; not having at that time an opinion of his own, he listened to his brother and changed his major from literature to medicine.

After having graduated from the preparatory school, he heard it said that the newest[20] university in Japan was located in N city, and moreover that N city was reputed to have the most beautiful women in Japan, so he requested a transfer to the university at N city.

---

[20]Probably Nagoya Gakuin University, founded in 1887 by an American Methodist minister.

Chapter 4: Nagoya

On the evening of August 29 in his twentieth year, he went by himself to the central railway station in Tokyo and took a night train headed for N city.

The sky that day looked like that of the first three or four days of the month in the old calendar; the firmament, indigo-violet colored, and sprinkled with stars, looked soft like swan's down. A half hint of a new moon hung obliquely in the western corner of the sky, looking like a Naiad's soft eyebrow, but with none of the appearance of blue-black mascara. All alone, he leaned against the window in the third-class car of the train and silently counted the lights in the windows of the houses that he passed. As the train plodded forward into the pitch-black night, and as that starlight of the metropolis grew more hazy, his mind suddenly gave rise to a myriad of sorrows and emotions, and he felt his eyes suddenly starting to grow warm.

"Sentimental, too sentimental!" he said out loud, wiped away his eyes, and then unexpectedly began to poke fun at himself.

"You don't even have a girlfriend whom you've left behind in Tokyo, you don't have any comrades or close friends who live there; when all is said and done, your tears are like something from outside yourself, like someone has splashed them there! Or does any of this have to do with your sad past life, or with the excess emotion you've felt for the last two years... but don't you normally say that you don't like Tokyo?

"Ah, one grows fond of a place after living there a year."

黃鶯住久渾相識，欲別頻啼四五聲！[21]

After he had let his imagination run wild for a while, then he quickly imagined himself being one of the Puritans as they first arrived in America.

"Those religious exiles, leaving their native shores, they must have been heroically tragic, emotionally distraught, like me."

As the train passed Yokohama, his feelings gradually began to die down. He sat numb for a moment, then he took out a postcard, and placing it on top of a book of Heinrich Heine's collected poetry, he used a lead pencil to write a poem to send to a friend in Tokyo.

> *A crescent moon high above the new willow*
>   *branches,*
> *Once again you leave your residence for a*
>   *faraway place.*
> *A four-walled pavilion, streaming flags: strife,*
>   *gambling, drink.*
> *Six distant street lamps, you follow them from the*
>   *train.*
> *You left home as a young man, confused, with few*

____

[21] "Black-naped orioles know each other after living together for a long time; when about to separate, they emit four or five weeping sounds repeatedly!" – Rong Yu (744-800 CE).

tears;
A poor home – in your luggage only old books.
Later, in the evening, tall reeds in limpid autumn
     waters,
Standing on the southern shore, you look for
     Pisces.[22]

In the dim light of the electric lamp, after sitting very quietly for a while, he began flipping through the pages of Heine's poetry again.

Lebet wohl, ihr glatten Saale,
Glatte Herren, glatte Frauen!
Auf die Berge will ich steigen,
Lachend auf euch niederschauen!
     – Heines "Harzreise"[23]

Frivolous world, ruthless men and women!
Yonder indistinct green mountain,
     want to fly on the wind,
And live there forever. From the very top of that
     peak,
Laughing, I will see you return whence you came,

---

[22]峨眉月上柳梢初，又向天涯別故居，

四壁旗亭爭睹酒，六街燈火遠隨車，

亂離年少無多淚，行李家貧只舊書，

後夜蘆根秋水長，憑君南浦覓雙魚。

[23]"Farewell you smooth halls, smooth men, smooth women! I want to climb up the mountain and look down on you, laughing. – Heine's 'Harzreise.'"

in the end.[24]

The monotonous sound of the wheels, a continuous repetitive sound reaching his ears, in less than thirty minutes this hypnotic sound of the train wheels had actually made him fall asleep, luring him into a dreamlike fairyland.

Early in the morning, at five o'clock, the sky gradually began to brighten. Looking out the window from the train, he saw only a thin line of blue sky wrapped in the color of evening. He poked his head out the window to have a better look, it was a landscape painting framed by a layer of mist; he thought: "As it turns out, today is yet another day of clear autumn weather, how truly blessed I am." After one hour, the steam-engine train arrived at the train station in N city.

Disembarking from the train, on the platform he met a Japanese student; he noticed two white lines on that student's hat, which told him that he was a student from the college he planned to attend. He approached the student, and, removing his hat, he asked him:

"Can you point me in the direction of the college?"

____

[24]Here is the protagonist's translation of Heine's stanzas:

浮薄的塵寰，無情的男女，

你看那隱隱的青山，我欲乘風飛去，

且住且住，

我將從那絕頂的高峰，笑看你終歸何處。

That student responded, saying:

"We can go there together."

So he rushed out of the train station together with that student, and in front of the station he boarded an electric tramcar.

It was still very early in the morning, the city's shop-keepers were not up yet. He rode the electric tramcar with that Japanese student, passing through the cold and cheerless streets and alleys until it passed in front of Crane Dance Park[25], where they got off. He asked the Japanese student:

"Is the school far from here still?"

"Still another two *li* or so by walking."

After having walked through the park, they went down a narrow road that ran through a series of rice paddies; he noticed the sun had already risen and dew drops were still hanging like pearls from the rice plants. A thicket of trees stood before them, and in the shade of the trees could be seen the rooves of several farmhouses. From two or three chimney stacks, rising above the farmhouses, escaped a faint wisp of smoke that floated into the early morning air. By the one or two wisps of that thin smoke that drifted towards him, carrying a fragrance of wood with them, he knew the farmers were already busy cooking their breakfasts on wood stoves.

When they reached the hotel near the school, he went inside to inquire about his luggage, sent over a week

---

[25]Crane Dance Park: 鶴舞公園, Hewu Gonyuan, in Nagoya.

earlier; it had arrived. As it turned out, that hotel had hosted foreign-exchange students from China before, consequently the proprietor treated him with respect. After having arrived at that hotel, he felt his prospects had a much more positive appearance to them.

But in spite of the reality of his present situation, he could not help, by the evening of the first day, poking fun at his hope for a brighter future. As it turns out, his hometown, back in China, was a very small town as well. After having arrived in Tokyo and having lived among the vast crowds of people there, although he often felt alone, nevertheless Tokyo's big city atmosphere was not yet completely out of keeping with the customs and practices he was used to from his childhood. Now, after having arrived in the country-side outside this N city, his hotel was a building standing all on its own, without a next-door neighbor in sight in any direction; just to the left of and beyond the front gate was the main road, on either side of which were rice paddies, and on the western edge of the property was a square-shaped reservoir full of wa-ter; moreover, since the school term had not yet start-ed, no students had arrived yet, and inside this vast hotel he was the only client. During the day he could deal with it alright, but when evening came, and when he opened his window to take a look outside, – there was nothing but pitch darkness in every direction; moreover, since everywhere outside N city was a large open field, there was nothing to block one's view, in any direction, when gazing out into the dis-tance; in the far-off distance were some lights, vari-able and flickering, that gave a dense ghostly atmos-phere to the scene. Also, in the ceiling above him, there were many insects and rodents; he stood in the center of his room, trembling, wondering if they were going to fall on him while they vied for food. Outside his window were several Chinese parasol trees; when the breeze moved their leaves, they made a soughing sound that went on endlessly; because his room was on the second floor, the shuddering sound of the leaves filled his ears. He began to grow frightened, and he almost wanted to cry. His homesickness (*nostalgia*) for the metropolis had never been so profound as on that night.

As soon as the school term started, he gradually acquired more friends. He felt his inborn, often intense temperament, towards the sky and the earth, towards the forests, fields, and rivers even – had relaxed. In less than six months, he had unexpectedly turned into a huge enthusiast of nature; it was all he could do to stand more than fifteen minutes apart from nature, so strong was his interest in it. His school was outside N city; and as just mentioned, everywhere outside that city was a large open plain; so the edges of the horizon extended vastly in all four directions. At that time, Japan's industry was not yet fully developed, and the population had not yet grown to the level it has at present, consequently near the school were many thickets and wide-open spaces, small hills and low mounds. Except for some small businesses that traded in writing instruments and study materials for students, as well as some restaurants, there were no inhabitants nearby. In this human wilderness, there was only a few hotels erected for students, like faint stars in a dawn sky, scattered and sown in the middle of the oat fields and melon patches. After dinner, he would throw a black woolen coat over his shoulders, choose a book he loved to read, and go on a carefree walk in the glow of the setting sun; this made him feel really happy. His interest in the countryside was probably also the result of a habit he had cultivated on these "Idyllic Wanderings."

When life was not one long fierce competition, when it was carefree and unrestrained, as during the Middle Ages, he felt even more suffering. His school textbooks, – he gradually began to abhor them; French novels from the school of Naturalism and those Chinese novels that are infamous for inciting lust and promoting licentiousness, – he read them over and over again, until he had almost memorized them.

Every now and then he produced a good poem; when that happened he felt really happy, and he knew his mental capacity was not yet damaged. When that happened, he made an oath to himself: "My mind still functions, it can still produce this kind of poetry; in the future I vow no longer to commit a sin. What's done is done, there's nothing I can do about it, but from now on I will never break a rule. If I make a fresh start from now on, my mind may still have a chance, maybe."

But when the urge to commit a sin came upon him, he forgot his oath again and again.

Every Thursday or Friday, or every twenty-sixth or twenty-seventh day of the month, a voracious desire to do whatever he pleased came over him. In his mind he thought, "next week or the beginning of next month, I will never sin again." Sometimes when Saturday evening or the end of the month rolled around again, he would go get a shave and take a bath, feeling that this would seal a new start, but after a few days had passed he couldn't stop consuming chicken eggs or drinking cow's milk again.

With these feelings of remorse and fear, unexpectedly one day he could not calm down, and his mental depression was also, from that moment forward, spinning out of control. This state of affairs lasted for one or two months; then the school year ended, and, in the ensuing two months of summer break, he suffered more than his usual dejection; by the time school started again, his two cheek bones had become more pronounced; the dark, ashen-grey color around his eyes was more accentuated; and his two bright pupils had changed: they looked like dead fish eyes.

Chapter 5: The Naked Eve

Autumn had rolled around again. A vast, deep blue sky expanded and grew higher day after day. The rice paddies next to his hotel, they all acquired a golden-yellow color. Cool breezes, morning and night, like a knife even, pierced men's heart and bones; the beautiful cold days of autumn and winter would soon be upon him.

It was one week earlier, in the afternoon, when he had taken a book of Wordsworth's poetry with him on the raised path between two fields and wandered half the day, footloose and fancy free.[26] From that day forward, his recurrent mental depression had never left him. It was only a few days earlier that he had met those two girl students on the road before his hotel; now, in general, his mood was usually very pure, when he was not living in close proximity to the common people of the street; in a quiet, calm, simple, and elegant location, he passed his days exactly as if in a dream. After he arrived in N city, in the blink of an eye, already a half a year or more had passed.[27]

---

[26]This refers back to the scene in chapter 1.

[27]The author's concept of time is a bit challenging and problematic in this story. For instance, in chapter 4 he had taken a train from Tokyo and arrived in Nagoya on August 30. Then he started school, soon got to summer break, and now it is autumn again. By now it is his second autumn in N city: it will have been one year, then, not half a year that he's in Nagoya. In the next paragraph it is spring already. But it's not just months, seasons and years, but also hours in a day, as we'll see later on in the

A warm south breeze blew day and night, the grass gradually became green again, and the grains of oat in the fields next to the hotel grew taller, inch by inch. Plants and animals all began to multiply; his depression, which had been handed down from generation to generation since the beginning of time, began to grow stronger with each passing day; in his bed, he committed a sin, and time and time again, he added to his accumulation of sin.

Originally he was the kind of person who prized refinement and cleanliness in people, but as soon as this wicked desire of his had developed, his intelligence was no match for it, his conscience became paralyzed; from childhood, he bore in mind the wise old adage that "The body's hair and skin must not be damaged," but, try as he may, he could not honor it. After having sinned, he bitterly and deeply repented it; gnashing his teeth, he said he would never do it again, but then two days later, all sorts of fantasy actively appeared and danced before his eyes. His usual emission involved imagining "Eve" appearing completely naked in front of him, to seduce him. The physical body of a middle-aged or older woman, in his mind, was more exciting to him than a virgin. His fits of depression, his fierce internal contests, – in the end, he was unable to get the better of them. This kind of thing, where the first time led to a second, and the second led to a third, and so on... became a habit for him. Each time after he committed a sin, he went

---

story, that are problematic. Either the author does this consciously – invoking the seasons and time that best reflect or affect the mood of his character, – or the narrator is intentionally unreliable.

to the library and flipped through the medical books; in the medical books were a thousand pages talking about the same thing: how this type of sin is harmful to the body. After reading this, the fear in his mind grew greater with each passing day. One day, – he didn't know where he got the information from, probably from a book, – he learned that 郭歌裡,[28] the modern Russian author, also had this same illness, and that he had died unexpectedly, unable to correct it; he thought that Gogol must have indulged himself because the author of "Dead Souls" was just like him. In any case, in spite of this small consolation, he always felt an extreme anxiety was building in his chest.

Because he loved cleanliness so much, everyday he always wanted to take a bath; because he was the kind of person who cherished his health a lot, every day he always wanted to consume some raw chicken eggs or drink cow's milk; but when he went to take a bath or drink cow's milk and raw chicken eggs, he always felt very ashamed afterwards because those were all things that bore testimony in his mind to his having sinned.

He felt his body become weak, and his ability to remember things diminish, with each passing day; also, gradually, the idea of looking into somebody's face developed into a kind of phobia with him; in his mind, when he saw a woman, he felt uneasy, it reminded him of that incident of before, that he was still a person who got red in the face. Recently, it did not matter where he went, he always felt ill at ease in a certain way. When he went to school, he thought his

----

[28] 郭歌裡: Gogol. In the original, these characters were in English.

Japanese classmates all seemed to reject him. For a long time he didn't seek out the few Chinese classmates that he knew, because when he came home after having gone out with them, he felt empty inside instead. Because the few Chinese classmates that he did have as friends were quite incapable of understanding what was going on in his head. When he went to call on them, he always wanted to get along with them, but after he had spent some time with them, and after a few words had been exchanged, he couldn't help regretting the mistake of calling on them again. Sometimes he had congenial conversations with his friends, then he allowed himself to warm up to some ideas for awhile; he revealed to his friends some of his private life, but on his return home, he regretted the indiscretion, and his heart reproached him for it; but, on the other hand, if he didn't go out and call on his friends, his life became even harder to bear. Consequently, of the few Chinese friends that he had, all of them said that he had acquired bad habits, that he was mentally disturbed. After he heard this kind of talk, towards those few Chinese classmates, just as towards the Japanese students, a desire for vengeance rose up in him. Day after day he drifted further and further away from his few Chinese classmates. From then on, whether on the street or in the classroom, whenever he ran into those several Chinese classmates of his, he didn't nod his head at them or acknowledge them at all. When there was a meeting of Chinese foreign-exchange students, of course he didn't attend. Thus he and his few compatriots had actually become just like two enemies.

Of all his Chinese classmates there was one person who was a very strange person, because of some moral sins in his marriage; so this friend of his particularly liked to focus on other people's scandals in his conversation, in order to cover up his own shortcomings; and this friend of his used to tell others that *he* was a mental case and repeated even the things he had told him in confidence.

After he had stopped seeking out friends, his loneliness nearly killed him; by good fortune, also staying at the hotel was the owner's daughter, who kept his mind occupied; otherwise he really could have killed himself. The hotel owner's daughter was seventeen years old, had a long face and very large eyes, and when she smiled one could see two small dimples on her cheeks and a gold-crowned tooth in her mouth; because she thought she had a really cute smile, she managed to smile often.

In his heart, although he really liked her, nevertheless when she brought him his meal or made his bed, he always assumed a kind of unapproachable attitude with her. Although he wanted to speak to her, as soon as he saw her, he could never open his mouth. When she entered his room, his breath grew short and he couldn't breathe. In her presence actually he suffered hardship, so now when she entered his room, he couldn't help but to leave. So although he treated her with respect, nevertheless he grew more and more interested in her with each passing day. One Saturday evening, the other students staying at the hotel had taken off on a walk to N city for entertainment. Because his financial situation was tight, as a result, after eating dinner, he went outside alone and walked around the pond on the west side of the hotel, then returned to the hotel and sat down by himself not doing anything.

After having sat down for a while, he thought he was alone on that vast and empty second floor. He calmly and quietly kept sitting there for a long while, when he finally grew impatient and thought about going outside again. Even though he intended to go outside, he couldn't help passing by the owner's door, because the owner and his daughter's room was next to the front door. He remembered that when he came in both the owner and his daughter were at supper eating. He thought of the suffering he would feel passing in front of her again, so he dropped the idea of going outside.

He took out a novel by G. Gissing, and after having read three or four poems in it, amidst the silence, suddenly he could hear the sound of tinkling water. He pricked up his ears to listen quietly, attentively, his breath becoming rapid in a split second, and his face red. He hesitated for a moment, then he softly opened the door of his room, taking care to pick up his slippers when he walked, and stealthily descended the staircase. Quietly opening the door to the privy, he used all his strength to lift himself up on his tiptoes and steal a glance through the glass window. As it turns out, the hotel's bathroom was next to the privy; through the privy's glass window one could see into the bathroom any activity that was going on. At first he thought he would take a quick peek and then go away, but after he had gotten a peek, it was if he had been nailed to the floor actually, and he could not move.

That pair of pointed breasts white as snow!

That pair of plump white thighs!

That curved line of her body!

He couldn't breathe, he was attentively watching for a while, when the muscles in his face started to convulse. The more he watched, the more difficult it became to deal with the shaking, and his forehead suddenly struck the window pane a little. Enveloped in vapor, the naked "Eve" with a lovable tone of voice called out: "Who's there?..."

He didn't make a sound, hastily ran out of the toilet, and hurriedly escaped upstairs.

He ran into his room, his face was hot and as if on fire, and his mouth was parched. First he gave himself a slap on the face, then he took out his bedding and went to bed. He tossed and turned in bed, never could fall asleep, then he pricked up his ears and heard the sound of voices downstairs. He listened closely, as the sound of splashing water stopped; after the bathroom door closed, he heard her footsteps as they seemed to come upstairs. Using the blanket to cover his head, he spoke to himself distinctly saying,

"She's told him! She's told him!"

That night, he never did fall asleep. The following day, early in the morning, at dawn, very scared and frightened he went downstairs. He washed his hands and face, brushed his teeth, took advantage of the fact that the owner and his daughter had not gotten up yet, and he exited the hotel as if escaping, and ran outside.

The dirt of the main road was moist with morning dew, no one had walked on it yet. The sun was just coming up. Indiscriminately, he made a beeline east; in the distance was a farmer, slowly pulling a cart full of wild vegetables. When he passed him, the farmer said to him suddenly: "Good Morning!"

He was startled, and then his face became flushed, in his chest his heart began beating rapidly, and he thought to himself: "Could it be that this farmer also knows?"

Without thinking, he ran for a long time; when he turned his head to look back at his school, it was already very far away; he looked up at the sky, the sun also had risen. He felt his fob, and tried to find his pocket watch to know what time it was, but that big silver onion, he hadn't brought it with him. From the angle of the sun, it looked like it was probably already nine o'clock in the morning more or less. Although he felt very hungry, nevertheless it didn't matter to him, he was still not willing to return to that hotel, to face the owner and his daughter. He considered going to buy a snack to allay his hunger, then he checked his pockets, and all that remained in them were one *jiao* two *fen*. He came to a country store, entered, and spent his one *jiao* two *fen* on some snacks, then thought about finding some place where he could eat them without anyone watching him. He walked until he came to a crossroads; he looked to the south and saw only the road crossing the road he had just come down, a north-south facing road, with very few people on it. In the southbound direction, the road sloped downwards, with high ramparts on either side, so he knew it was cut out of, and coming down from, a hill. That road he had just come along was the main road, on the top of a ridge, with the road crossing it, going through the center of it, and descending on either side. He hesitated at the crossroads, at the top of that hill, for a long while, until he decided finally to take the southbound road that descended. Beyond the two ramparts, he could see that the road opened up, passed through a large plain, and continued on straight to the further limits of the city. At the other end of the plain was a thicket of trees, right in the middle, under a deep blue sky, and he thought to himself:

"That must be A temple."[29]

After having walked down the round and put the two tall ramparts behind him, he glanced to his left and saw an inclined plain, which went up to the top of a hill that was surmounted by a parapet; around it were some cottages, on the doors of each of which hung a horizontal board with three characters inscribed on it: "香雪海"[30]. He got off the road and walked up the hill until he reached the wall of the parapet; he pushed on the gate gently, and the two doors made of brushwood opened suddenly. He then casually stepped inside. Inside the gate was a meandering path, which led farther up the inclined plane to the top of the hill. On

---

[29]Atsuta Shrine, 熱田神宮, in Nagoya.

[30]香雪海: Sea of fragrant snow – a reference to how the garden looks when all the plum trees are in full bloom.

both sides of the meandering path were many old, dark-green Japanese plum trees. He knew then that this was the plum tree orchard. He followed the meandering path, and, across the northern approach, when he arrived at the top of the hill, a level stretch of landscape unfolded before him like a painting. This orchard extended from the base of the hill all the way up it, straddling the inclined surface of the southern-facing hill, to the level ground at the summit, where he stood, creating an exceptionally serene and elegant setting.

There was a precipice that was a thousand *ren*[31] long on the western edge of the level ground at the top of the hill; opposite the precipice, between two cliffs, was the very same north-south road he had just walked along. A large multi-story house and several flat, single-story houses were built at the top of the precipice. Because the windows and doors of these houses were all shut, he was certain that they served for selling food and drink on the days of the plum blossom festival. In front of the large house was some turf in the middle of which stood several square, white stones that surrounded a small garden; in the middle of the garden stood an old plum tree; at the southern-most extremity of that turf, there where the level hilltop was about to plunge downwards, a stone tablet was erected, recording the history of this plum orchard. He sat down on the grass in front of that stone tablet and ate his snack.

After eating, he stretched out his legs and sat on the

---

[31]ren: (仞) a measure of length or depth, equal to eight feet approximately.

grass for a while. There was no sound of people from any direction; occasionally he could hear the sound of one or two birds twittering from some branches in the distance. He lifted his eyes and looked up at the limpid blue sky, toward that shining disk in the sky, and he thought that everything around him, the houses made of sticks, the small birds, the grass, everything was peaceful in the warm sunlight, naturally receiving nature's nourishment. The sin of yesterday evening was a faint recollection now, just like the image of some sail far out at sea, – he didn't know where it had disappeared to.

This plum orchard's level ground and inclined plane were crisscrossed by many meandering paths. He stood up and walked up and down the paths for a while, and then he noticed still another single-story house built right in the middle of the plum trees on the inclined plane. Several paces to the east of this structure was an old well, buried under a pile of pine needles. He cranked the pump on the top of the well, which clinked and clanked, but no water came out. He thought:

"They probably open this park only when the plum trees are in bloom; at all other times nobody lives here."

And he spoke to himself again saying:

"Given this place is empty, why don't I go find the owner and ask if I can't lodge here for a spell." Having fixed on this idea, he then ran down the hill and intended to find the owner of the garden. Reaching the gate, he bumped right into a fifty-year old farmer who was just then entering the park. He apologized to the farmer, and then he asked him:

"Whose park is this, do you happen to know?"

"I'm in charge of it."

"Where do you live?"

"I live on the other side of the road."

As he said this, the peasant indicated with his finger the road leading to his house. He looked to the west: sure enough, at the very end of the western rampart was a place where his small house stood. He nodded his head, and then he asked:

"Could I rent one of the multi-storied houses in the park to live in for a while?"

"Yes, but just one person?"

"Just me."

"Then no need."

"What do you mean?"

"You students have moved in before, multiple times; however, probably because of the quiet, you don't stay more than ten days, then move out again."

"I can live on my own, you can rent to me; I'm not afraid of the quiet."

"If that's the case, I see no reason not to rent to you; when do you want to move in?"

"This afternoon."

"Alright, no problem."

"Please sweep it clean and neat for me, so I'm not anxious after moving in."

"Will do. Until we meet again!"

"Until we meet again!"

Chapter 6: Depression

After having moved into the plum orchard on the hill, his depression began to take a turn for the worse.

A disagreement arose suddenly between him and his eldest brother in Beijing, on account of some small matter. He wrote a very long letter to him, in which he severed their relationship.

After mailing that letter, he spent a lot of his time staring blankly out over the grass plot in front of the house he was renting. As he thought more deeply about it, he actually believed himself to be the most miserable man on earth. In fact, this time the rupture was his own doing. The internecine strife had more to do with a dispute over their family name than anything else, consequently he hated his brother like a serpent or scorpion. When others bullied him, he would always take it out on his brother like this:

"How can I find fault with others, when my own brother even acts in this way!"

He always came to the same conclusion, utterly exhausted by his brother's harsh treatment, as little memories started coming back to him. He listed them all out, all kinds of past deeds his brother had done, and his verdict was that his brother was an evil person, and that he himself was a good person. He also came up with a list of his own good points, and an exaggerated list of the things he had suffered. When he had proven to himself that he was the world's most miserable person, the tears started to come down like waterfalls. While he sobbed to himself, a kind of softness seemed to permeate the air, and a voice said to him:

"Oh, is it you who's crying? That truly is an injustice. It looks as though you're that kind of good person who endures people's maltreatment, this truly is an injustice. Stop it, stop it, this is also heaven's mandate, you should stop crying right now, for fear you might hurt your body!"

In his mind, he heard this voice speaking, and then he became entirely happy. He felt that amidst the sorrow was a kind of boundless sweetness also.

Because he wanted to retaliate against his brother's hatred, he dropped the study of medicine and changed his major to literature; his idea being that medicine was his brother's idea, and that to change his major back to literature would be a clear declaration of war on his brother. Besides, changing his major from medicine to literature would add another year of study, meaning that it would delay his graduation from the university by one year. He thought to himself that "to extend your studies by one year, that means to die earlier by one year; the earlier you are able to die, the better your chances of holding onto the enmity with your brother forever." He was afraid that after one or two years, the two brothers' feelings would have softened and that they would have reconciled with each other by then; this change of major back to literature would be the right way to perpetuate the hostility.

The weather gradually grew very cold; one month had passed since he had moved onto the hill, and already there were several days of gloomy weather, with ashen gray stratus clouds hanging in the air daily. When the north wind began to blow, each cold gust made the leaves on the plum trees fall. When he had first moved in, he had sold some old books and bought many cooking implements, thinking to make his own meals for a month; but because the weather had gotten colder, he didn't feel like cooking anymore. His left the preparation of his meals to the gardener's family down the hill, and received a packet of food everyday, so that he was living his life like an idle monk who had recently left the monastery; apart from complaining about others and scolding himself often, he had nothing else to do.

One day, he got up very early in the morning, and after having opened the windows facing east, he saw before him, on the horizon, several wisps of red cloud floating in the sky. Early dawn yet, the half circle of the eastern sky shone a kind of silvery-red, ashen-gray color. Because it had rained lightly all day the day before, when he saw this clear sky at dawn, it instilled in him a great happiness, compared to an ordinary day. He walked along the hill's inclined plane, and after having washed his hands and face at the old well where he drew his water, he felt full of energy; in a single instant, he looked his old self again. Then he ran back up the hill to his house, to grab a volume of Huang Zhongze's poetry from off the shelf, and recited it aloud while walking hurriedly along the plum orchard paths, up and down and all around. It didn't take long before the sun had risen.

From the hilltop where he lived, he looked out in a southerly direction, and he could make out a large field below. The rice in the field had not yet been harvested: it was a golden-yellow color, because of the purple-green backdrop of the sky, reflecting the sun's dawning light, – the scene looked just like a still life painting by Millet.[32] He felt that he had already somehow changed in manner and appearance, like an early Christian of several thousand years earlier, before this revelation of nature; unconsciously, he started chuckling at his narrow-mindedness.

"Forgiven! Forgiven! You common folk who have sinned against me, I forgive you all; come, come hither, all of you, come hither and make peace!" In his hand he was holding that collection of poetry, in his eyes two pools of limpid tears were quivering, just opposite that field of autumn colors; and while he was standing silently there thinking these things, he heard two people very nearby, speaking in soft whispers, saying:

"You really must come this evening!" It was clearly a man's voice.

"I really want to come, but I'm afraid that..."

Once he heard that girl's sweet voice, it was as if he had been electrified; he thought his blood had stopped circulating. As it turns out, he was standing just to the right of a tall cluster of grass; that couple was on the other side of it, so they didn't know he was there, listening to them. The man continued speaking:

---

[32]Millet: Jean-François Millet (AD 1814-1875), a French painter known for his depictions of rural life.

"You really are a nice girl, a fine girl; please come this evening; until now we haven't slept together..."

He suddenly heard the sound of two people's lips, a kind of fervid sucking sound.

He looked like a feral dog ready to steal some food, frozen with fear, leaning over in order to listen. "You're going to hell, you're going to hell, how can you sink so low!" he thought to himself

Although he was scolding himself like this in his mind, his two ears pricked up, for he didn't want to miss a single word, he was so completely caught up in listening to them.

The sound of bodies rustling in the leaves, on the ground.

The sound of clothes coming loose.

The sound of a man's deep breathing.

The sound of French kissing.

The woman's half gentle, half serious, inarticulate voice:

"You!... You!... Quick!... Do it, quick!... Don't... Don't.... Don't... people.... people... can see."

His face suddenly turned an ashen-gray color. His eyes grew red like fire. His jaw was clacking up and down. He wanted to get up and run away, but he could not; his mind gave the command, but his two legs didn't obey. For a long time afterwards, after they had gotten up and dressed and gone away, he felt depressed. And then like a wet cat or half-drowned dog, he dragged himself back to the house, took out his bedding, and went straight to sleep.

Chapter 7: The Japanese Tavern

He hadn't eaten anything for lunch; he slept right through it until four o'clock in the afternoon, when he finally got up. At that time, the sun was starting to go down, bathing everything, far and near, in its light. At the other end of the plain, a dark blue girdle of mist gently flowed in and enveloped the woods. He staggered down the hill and got on to that north-south-running public road, the one that passed through the plain, and without thinking too much about it, he headed south. He put the plain behind him and reached the temple, where there was a stop; he waited for the tramcar. When the tramcar arrived, coming from the south, he got on it without thinking, not knowing why he wanted to get on it nor where that car would take him.

After fifteen or sixteen minutes, it stopped; he was told to switch tramcars, so he switched tramcars. Another twenty or thirty minutes later, the tramcar stopped again; he heard the operator call out that this was the end of the line, so he got off. In front of him was the port of Zhugang (築港).

Before him lay a portion of the sea's vast body of water, reflecting the late afternoon sunlight, smiling at him. Across the water and to the south was a line of green hills, faintly floating in the transparent air, on the western edge of which was a long dike, going straight through the heart of the bay. Beyond the dike, a lighthouse was situated, standing like a giant. Several empty ships and sampan, moored there, floated on the water. In the middle of the water, along the shore, were many buoys, subject to the light of the sun as it went down, dark red and slanting. From afar, the wind rose, carrying with it several monotonous snatches of conversation, it wasn't clear in what language, and he also wasn't certain from which direction they came.

He walked aimlessly on the shore, until all of a sudden he heard a peal of chimes. He ran to look; actually it was a ferry that had issued them, serving as a call to board. He stood there for a while, watching as a steamboat approached from the opposite shore. Immediately afterwards, he and a forty- or fifty-year old worker boarded that steamboat and sat down.

After crossing to the eastern shore and disembarking, he advanced several paces, until he came to a large building close to the shore. It had large doors, inside the front courtyard of which was a rock garden with flowers and plants, well-kept and lovely to behold. Without thinking whether it was right or wrong, he strolled inside. Not even a few paces inside, he suddenly heard from inside the front of the building a woman's sweet voice calling out to him, saying:

"Come inside, please!"

He was slightly startled naturally, then dumbly just stood there, in his head thinking:

"This must be a tavern, but I have heard that in such a place as this there is always a prostitute."

As he was considering this, he became aroused, as if a bucket of cold water had been dumped on him. Then his expression immediately changed. He wanted to go inside but he couldn't. He wanted to go away but he couldn't. How pathetic he was, with the courage of a rabbit and the wantonness of monkeys and apes, all of a sudden caught in a trap that was difficult to escape.

"Come inside! Come inside, please!"

From within, a drippingly sweet voice called out to him again, with a hint of laughter in it.

"Vile thing, you have the cheek to take advantage of me and my timidity?" he thought to himself.

Growing angry in this fashion, his face turned red as if warmed in a fire. Clenching his teeth, lightly dragging his feet, tightening his hands into fists, he walked forward and in, in a straight line toward those young hostesses as if to wage battle. But that look on his face, his complexion, natural one moment, red the next, and the very slight twitching of muscles in his face, – he was not entirely able to conceal it. When he walked up to the hostesses, he nearly started crying like a child.

"Come upstairs, please!"

"Come upstairs, please!"

He tightened his scalp and followed a seventeen- or eighteen-year-old hostess upstairs, at which time his mind had already calmed down a bit. After taking a few steps, after he had passed through a secret passage, a pungent burst of fragrance, the kind of fragrance of flesh that is characteristic of Japanese women, together with the odor of sesame-seed oil in their hair, penetrated his nostrils with a humph! He immediately began to feel dizzy, his eyes started to see stars, and it seemed to him as if he was about to fall backwards. He then took another look, and in front of him, in the middle of the darkness, was another woman's long round powdered face, smiling at him, asking:

"Hey! You want to go to some place with a view of the sea? Or what?"

He felt the woman's disgorged breath warm his face up, with a humph! He unconsciously inhaled a mouthful of it, deeply. When he became aware of this behavior of his, his face immediately turned red. He had no choice but to reply to her, vaguely saying:

"Let's go some place with a view of the sea."

When they entered that small room with a view of the sea, the hostess then asked him what kind of food he wanted to eat. He then responded:

"Anything will do."

"Alcohol?"

"Yes."

After the hostess had left the room, he got up and pushed open the paper window to let a gust of fresh air in. Because the air in the room was very heavy and turbid, and the fragrance of the woman he had just gotten a whiff of in the narrow passage was still hanging in the air in the room, he felt really oppressed by it.

A large bay calmly floated before his eyes. A breeze seemed to start up, blowing, and wave after wave on the sea, taking in the reflection of the sun, shimmered like golden fish and fish scales. He stood at the window gazing out for a while, softly reciting a line of poetry: "The setting sun was red on the seaside houses."[33]

He gazed off to the west and saw the sun far away on the southwest horizon just one *zhang* in height. He gazed at it dumbly for a while, his thoughts still tied up with that hostess of earlier. From inside her mouth, on her head, in her face, and on her body, the fragrance wouldn't let him think of anything else. He knew too well that his mind's desire to recite poetry was fake, and that his thoughts of the woman's body were real.

After a while, that hostess shifted back into the room with food and drink, kneeled down before him, and affectionately offered him some rice wine. He wanted to take a careful look at her in his mind, to tell her how low he was feeling, but his eyes somehow didn't dare look straight into hers, and the back of his tongue somehow was unable to move. He was no more than a mute, and he stole a glance at her delicate and soft white hands resting in her lap, with the inner stitching of a corner of her pink apron exposed.

As it turns out, Japanese women don't wear underpants; they wrap a very short apron tightly around

---

[33]The setting sun was red on the seaside houses: 夕陽紅上海邊樓.

their body's flesh. On the exterior is a long sleeve of clothing, which has no buttons or fasteners on it, and a belt that is a *chi* or so wide is merely tied around the waist, at the back, into a square knot. When they walk, the front of their clothing lifts open with each step they take, so one can always catch a glimpse of the red apron with the white plump flesh of their legs. This is the special beauty of Japanese women. When he meets a female on the street or highway, he pays attention to that area. While gnashing his teeth, he reprimands himself sorely, "brute! treacherous dog! abject coward!" just like that.

He looked at the corner of that hostess's apron, and his heart started beating wildly. The more he wanted to speak with her, the more he felt unable to say a word. She probably got a little impatient, for she asked him softly:

"Where do you live?"

As soon as he heard her say this, his lean, pale face flushed red. Ineffectually by way of response, ever haltingly, he was unable to get the words out clearly. Pathetic, he just stood there on the scaffold.

Actually, Japanese people despise Chinese people, just as we despise pigs and dogs. Japanese people all call us "Chinaman," – these three syllables, "Chinaman," in Japanese, is like our calling someone contemptuously a "dirty thief," but it sounds worse; now, in front of this beautiful young lady, he couldn't help responding, resignedly, with this: "I am a 'Chinaman.'"

China, oh China, how is it you don't grow big and strong!

His whole body began to shake, and tears started to roll down his face.

That hostess watched him as he shook violently, and then she encouraged him to drink some of the rice wine by himself; thinking that it would help him to calm his nerves, she then said:

"The rice wine is almost finished, I'll go get another bottle, okay?"

She left the room, and he stopped shaking after a stretch; then he heard the sound of that hostess's footsteps coming back up the stairs. He thought for sure she was going to come into his room, so he straightened up his clothes a bit, corrected his posture. But she deceived him. In fact, she was leading two or three other guests to the room next door. Those two or three guests were all teasing her, and she responded sweetly to them with this:

"Don't make trouble now; next door there's another guest."

He heard them then and immediately started to grow angry. In his mind, he scolded them:

"Dirty dogs! Vulgar animals! You dare come here and bully me? Vengeance, vengeance, I will always want to exact vengeance on you. Where in this world is there a sincere girl! That heartless thing of a hostess, you have the impertinence to cast me aside? That's it, that's it, I will never love women again, I will never love women again. I love just my motherland, I will take my motherland for a lover."

He immediately considered returning home and applying himself seriously to his studies. But in his heart, he envied those bastards in the room next door. There was still a place in his heart where he hoped that that hostess would come back into his room.

He contained his anger, and in silence he knocked back several cups of rice wine which made his body grow warm. He opened the window again, and he saw the sun on the verge of setting. Several more cups of rice wine in succession and he felt that the seascape before him had become hazy. Beyond the western dike, the lighthouse's shadow had grown very long. There was an obscure layer of mist, where the sky blended with the sea; behind this layer, like a murky and turbid veil or gauze, the sun hesitated in the western sky and appeared reluctant to go down. He watched it for a long while, and he didn't know why, but he found it laughable. "He-he," he chuckled, and then with his hand he touched his cheeks which felt as if they were on fire; then, talking to himself, he said:

"You're drunk!"

That hostess eventually came back into the room. Seeing his red face, seeing him standing there before the open window smiling like an imbecile, she asked:

"Aren't you cold with the window open like that?"

"It's not cold; this beautiful dying light, who doesn't want to look at it?"

"You really are a poet! I brought more wine."

"A poet! I am a poet actually. Go fetch me a pencil and paper, I'll write a poem for you to read."

After the hostess went out, he felt that he was starting to act strange. He thought, "How can I be so courageous all of a sudden?"

He knocked back several more cups of the hot rice wine she had just brought in, and, feeling even happier, he couldn't help laughing out loud again. He heard the vulgar men in the room next door starting to sing Japanese songs loudly, and then he magnified his voice while singing:

> *Drunk, patting the railing, feeling smashed and*
> *   cold.*
> *Rivers and lakes, few and far between; winter*
> *   again, brutal.*
> *The acutely pitiful parrot, backbone of China old,*
> *Has had no appointment yet as a Changsha*
> *   official.*
>
> *One meal, one thousand gold coins; a scheme for*
> *   just rewards[34].*
> *Several men, five belches, difficult to tune out.*
> *Boundless misty water, I turn my head towards*
> *Cathay, O Cathay! my hidden tears shoot out.[35]*

---

[34]Just rewards: in other words, revenge.

[35] 「醉拍闌 ，江湖寥落又冬殘，
劇憐鸚鵡中州骨，未拜長沙太傅宮，
一飯千金圖報易，幾人五噫出關難，
茫茫煙水回頭望，也為神州淚暗彈。」

He recited this poem loudly, several times, then he fell back drunk on the mat.

Chapter 8: Motherland, Oh Motherland!

When he sobered up, he found himself sleeping under a thin, red silk blanket, which had a strange fragrance to it. The room he was in was not very large, and it was no longer lit by daylight. In the middle of it was suspended a ten-candela electric bulb. Next to the pillow was arranged a pot of tea and two teacups. After gulping down two or three cups of tea, he got up and staggered to the door, which he opened, when right at that moment the hostess of earlier in the day ran up to him. She said to him:

"Hey, so you woke up?"

He nodded his head, smiling faintly, and said:

"Yes. Where is the toilet exactly?"

"I'll show you."

Then he followed her. When he walked with her through that narrow passageway it was like daylight, the electric lights lit it up very bright. Somewhere far away he could hear the sound of songs, three-stringed instruments, and loud laughter. The things that had happened earlier in the day, he began to remember them. He recalled getting drunk, and when he remembered the things he had said to the hostess, he felt his face grow flushed.

After having visited the toilet and returning to the room, he asked that girl:

"Is this blanket yours?"

The girl smiled:

"Yes."

"What time is it now?"

"About eight forty or so."

"Go get the bill."

"Okay."

He paid the bill in full and handed a banknote to the hostess, as a tip, his hand trembling a little. The hostess said: "I really don't want it."

He knew she would dislike it, given it was so small an amount. His face became red again. He reached into his pocket and found he had only one other banknote. He took it out and gave it to her, saying, "Don't refuse. Please take it."

His hand was trembling even more violently than before, and his voice began to tremble as well. The girl shot him a glance, and then in a low voice she said, "Thank you!"

He ran down the stairs, slipped on his leather shoes, then walked outside.

Once outside, it was extremely cold; the day felt like the first eighth or ninth day of the month, of the old calendar; a cold half moon was suspended high in the sky on his left. The thin, blue semi-circular canopy of the sky had a few scattered stars in it, here and there.

He walked along the seashore for a while, looking at the fisherman's lights on the distant shore, like will-o'-the-wisps luring him on. The golden light of the moon was reflected on the waves, and they seemed like an elemental spirit's fluid glance, opening and closing – winking at him. Not knowing why, he suddenly thought of jumping into the sea to drown himself.

He felt his pockets and sides to see whether he had any money for the electric tram, but he didn't. Thinking again about what he had done that day, he couldn't help reprimanding himself.

"How in the world could I have gone to that place? In a short period of time, I have turned into one of the lowest sorts of people. To regret, but not enough; to regret, but not nearly enough. I will die here then. The love I seek probably doesn't exist. A life without love – is it any different than a kind of death? My god, this dull and dry life, this dull and dry life, so many people on earth looking at me with hatred, bullying me, including my oldest brother, my own flesh and blood, everyone pushing me in this direction, to the point of leaving the world behind. How will I make a living, and how will I survive in such a hard, cruel world!"

Having thought this, he began to weep, the tears flowing continuously down his cheeks. That ashen-colored face of his was not much different from that of a dead person's. He made no attempt to wipe away the tears, and the moonlight fell on his face and made the two lines of tears look like morning dew on a leaf reflecting the light. He turned his head to look back on his long, thin shadow, and he felt heartache.

"How pitiable you are, you pure and faithful shadow, you have followed me around these twenty-one odd years, and today this large sea will be your grave; my body, although humiliated by others, I really should not have abused you, as weak and thin as you are, to have brought you to this point. Shadow, oh shadow, forgive me!"

He looked to the west at the light from the lighthouse, turning red one moment, green the next, doing what it is supposed to do. When the green light reflected on the sea, the surface of the water revealed a faint, natural, green-colored path. Looking again into the distance, he focused his gaze on the point just beneath that faint blue western sky where a bright star was shuddering.

"Just beneath that uncertain, shuddering bright star is my old country. It is also my land of birth. Beneath that star, I once spent eighteen autumns and winters; my native soil! Now I am unable see your face again."

While he walked, he used these words of self-pity, self-mourning, and heart-broken feeling.

Having continued to walk for a while, he again cast a glance at that bright star in the west, and his tears, like a rain shower, started falling. He thought the scenery in every direction began to look blurry and indistinct. He wiped his tears away, stopped walking, let out a long sigh, and then said stammeringly:

"Motherland, Oh motherland! My death is your fault!

"Hurry up and grow rich! Grow strong!

"You have many sons and daughters suffering hardship!"

Other Books by the Publisher

Fanchette's Pretty Little Foot by Restif de La Bretonne

Je M'Accuse... by Léon Bloy

My Hospitals & My Prisons by Paul Verlaine

Salvation Through the Jews by Léon Bloy

Words of a Demolitions Contractor by Léon Bloy

Cellulely by Paul Verlaine

Ecclesiastical Laurels by Jacques Rochette de la Morlière

Flowers of Bitumen by Émile Goudeau

Songs for Her & Odes in Her Honor by Paul Verlaine

On Huysmans' Tomb by Léon Bloy

Ten Years a Bohemian by Émile Goudeau

The Soul of Napoleon by Léon Bloy

Blood of the Poor by Léon Bloy

Joan of Arc and Germany by Léon Bloy

A Platonic Love by Paul Alexis

The Revealer of the Globe: Christopher Columbus & His Future Beatification (Part One) by Léon Bloy

An Immodest Proposal by Dr. Helmut Schleppend

The Pornographer by Restif de La Bretonne

Style (Theory and History) by Ernest Hello

On the Threshold of the Apocalypse: 1913-1915 by Léon Bloy

She Who Weeps (Our Lady of La Salette) by Léon Bloy

The Sylph by Claude Prosper Jolyot de Crébillon (*fils*)

Voyage in France by a Frenchman by Paul Verlaine

Ourigan, Oregon by William Clark, Richard Robinson, and anonymous

Drowning by Yu Dafu

Cull of April by Francis Vielé-Griffin

The Misfortune of Monsieur Fraque by Paul Alexis

Fêtes Galantes & Songs Without Words by Paul Verlaine

Joys by Francis Vielé-Griffin

The Son of Louis XVI by Léon Bloy

Septentrion by Jean Raspail

The Resurrection of Villiers de l'Isle-Adam by Léon Bloy

Poems Saturnian by Paul Verlaine

The Biography of Léon Bloy: Memories of a Friend by René Martineau

Fredegund, France: A Book of Poetry by Richard Robinson

The Good Song by Paul Verlaine

Swans by Francis Vielé-Griffin

Constantinople and Byzantium by Léon Bloy

Enamels and Cameos by Théophile Gautier

Four Years of Captivity in Cochons-sur-Marne: 1900-1904 by Léon Bloy

Dark Minerva: Prolegomena: The Moral Construction of Dante's Divine Comedy by Giovanni Pascoli

What is Fascism: Discourses and Polemics by Giovanni Gentile

The Desperate Man by Léon Bloy

Meditations of a Solitary in 1916 by Léon Bloy

The Ride of Yeldis & Other Poems by Francis Vielé-Griffin

Silvie & The Chimeras by Gérard de Nerval

Italian Nationalism by Enrico Corradini

www.ingramcontent.com/pod-product-compliance
Lightning Source LLC
Chambersburg PA
CBHW030841200726
48285CB00007B/2504